To all the teddy bears, blankies, Baby Kays, and other comforts of the world
—T.L.

"I am who I am because somebody loved me." —Dr. Cornell West
Grateful for all who have spread wide their arms, especially Mom and Dad
—J.R.-Z.

Text copyright © 2020 by Tom Lichtenheld
Illustrations copyright © 2020 by Julie Rowan-Zoch

hmhbooks.com

The illustrations in this book were done in Procreate on an iPad.
The text type was set in a font based on Julie Rowan-Zoch's handwriting.
The display type was hand lettered by Julie Rowan-Zoch.
Book design by Celeste Knudsen

Library of Congress Cataloging-in-Publication Data

Names: Lichtenheld, Tom, author. | Rowan-Zoch, Julie, illustrator.
Title: Louis / Tom Lichtenheld ; illustrated by Julie Rowan-Zoch.
Description: Boston : Houghton Mifflin Harcourt, [2020] | Audience: Ages 4
  to 7. | Audience: Grades K—1. | Summary: Tired of the "dangerous
  adventures" with his human boy, a teddy bear decides to run away but
  reconsiders when bedtime arrives.
Identifiers: LCCN 2019039908 | ISBN 9781328498069 (hardcover)
Subjects: CYAC: Teddy bears—Fiction.
Classification: LCC PZ7.L592 Lo 2020 | DDC [E]—dc23
LC record available at https://lccn.loc.gov/2019039908

Manufactured in China
SCP 10 9 8 7 6 5 4 3 2 1
4500799711

LOUIS

TOM LICHTENHELD

ILLUSTRATED BY

JULIE ROWAN-ZOCH

HOUGHTON MIFFLIN HARCOURT
BOSTON   NEW YORK

From day one . . .

I've been a pillow . . .

a hankie . . .

and lunch for a prehistoric beast.

I've been buried alive . . .

thrown into a hurricane . . .

and hung out to dry.

I've been left to the mercy
of wild animals . . .

poked by needles . . .

and made an accessory to a crime.

I've been x-rayed . . .

milk-sprayed . . .

and mislaid.

I can bear it no longer.

The next time this kid squeezes me, I'm outta here.

Well, no sense running away in the rain.

But as soon as little sister wraps up this party,

I'm packing my bags.

Meanwhile, I need to build up my strength for the getaway.

Seriously, right after we do
our show-and-tell routine,

1 brave bear

I'm history.

I know, I know . . .
we're awesome.

Okay, this is perfect.
The minute that light goes out,

I'm off like a dirty shirt . . .
making like a tree and leaving.

Okay, now!

"C'mon, Louis, you silly bear."

On second thought . . .

a bear could do worse.

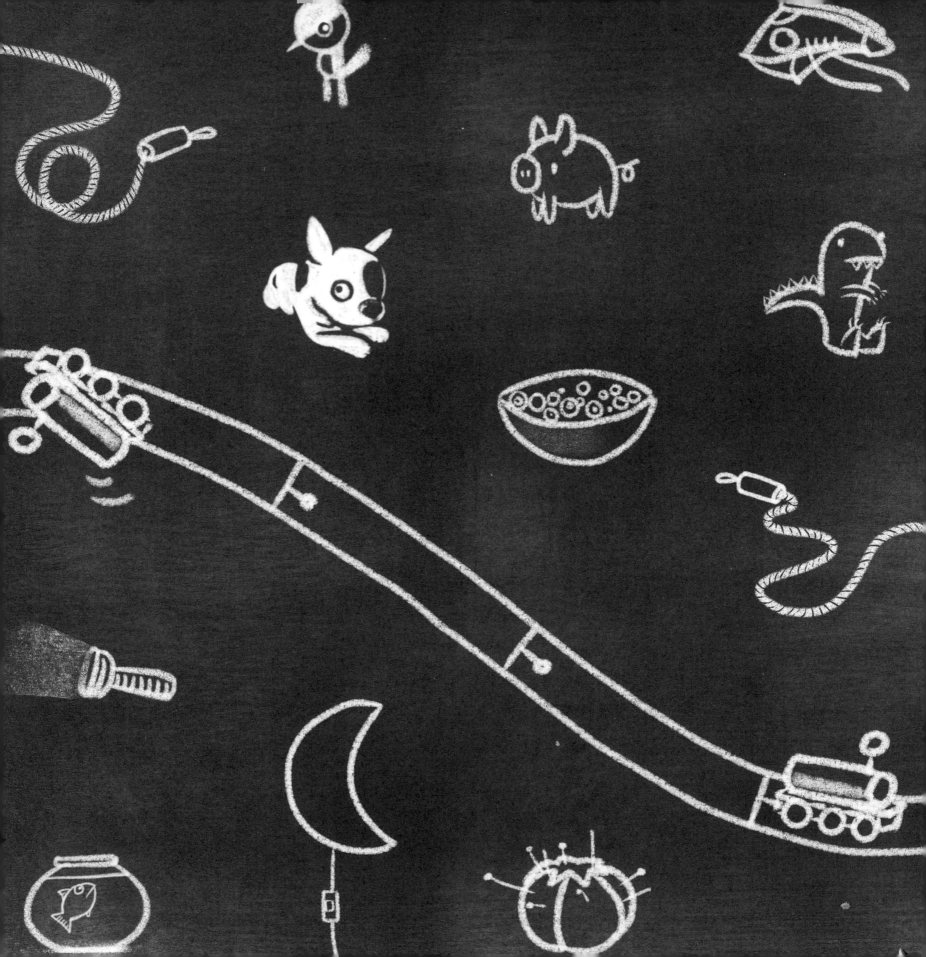